FLASH GORDON

THE ICE MONSTER

by Al Williamson

A Tom Doherty Associates Book

ISBN: 523-41333-5

A Tom Doherty Associates Original

Printed in the United States of America

A rocketship skims above Tropica, on the planet Mongo. Flash Gordon is at the controls. With him are his sweetheart, Dale Arden, and his good friend, the great scientist, Dr. Hans Alexis Zarkov...

Al
Williamson

We must get to Mingo City and finish our mission for Earth.
Yes, Flash. We've been helping other people here on Mongo for so long that I nearly forgot our mission for our own planet.

Well, kids, we shouldn't have any trouble now. The weather is clear. We'll be there in a few hours.

As the three leave Tropica, Flash's thoughts turn back to the day he first heard of this strange planet... shortly after his graduation from Yale...

People of Earth feared that a newly-sighted planet would eventually collide with Earth!

As they neared Mongo, they lost control of the ship. They crash-landed in the empire of ***Ming the Merciless,*** self-proclaimed emperor of Mongo, who tried to put them in prison!

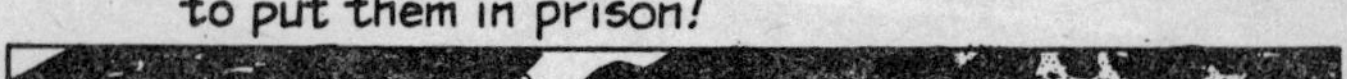

Flash and his companions managed to escape from Ming with the help of the rightful ruler, King Barin, and his beautiful wife, Queen Aura, Ming's daughter.

Among the others who helped Flash in his attempt to overthrow Ming were King Vultan and his hawkmen...

...Azura, the Witch Queen...

...The underwater people of Queen Undina...

...And in Frigia, the land to the north, Queen Fria and her husband Ronal, cousin of King Barin.

After several years of bloody war, Ming's power was at last broken.

Leaving King Barin in command, the three returned to Earth. They gave the United States many secrets of Mongo science which would help to restore peace. Flash was given the military rank of colonel.

A serious problem developed...The secrets of Mongo science needed huge quantities of radium. The mineral was plentiful on Mongo. So the three set out again for Mongo--only to crash upon the continent of Tropica!

Here they helped Queen Desira, whose throne had been seized by a tyrant.

Look, Flash! A land that is not charted on the maps... Let's explore it!

Oh, no you don't, Zarkov! Remember our mission.
Dale's right, Doc. We must get radium for Earth.

There it is, Flash..., Mingo City! AT LAST! I can see a lot of changes since we left.
It seems peaceful under Barin's leadership.

King Barin and Queen Aura welcome them with joy.

Several days later...
Say hello to Fria and Ronal for me, Flash. I will have our new rocketship ready when you get back.
Good old Doc. You've *never* failed us!

Meanwhile, in Frigia...
Ronal... We must have a party to welcome our good friends.

And evil plans are shaken,... ...

Flash, I have already arranged to get the radium you need. My men will have it ready in a few days.
Thanks, Ronal, now we can relax and enjoy your welcome.

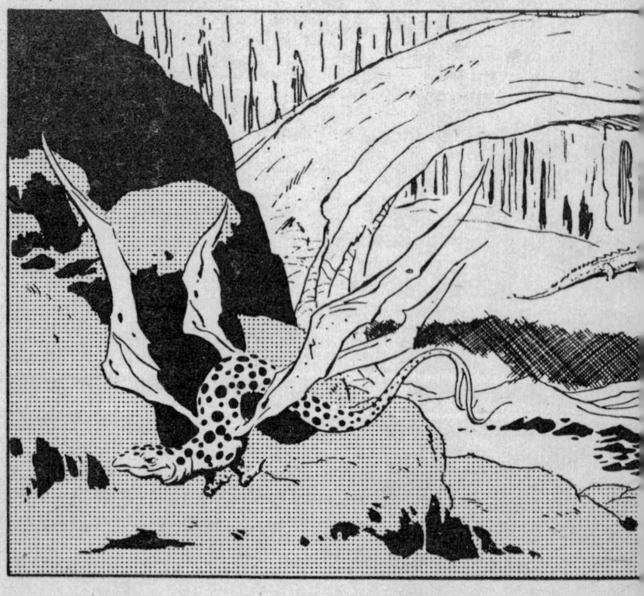

The next day, Queen Fria and Ronal arrange a hunt in the white lands of Frigia.

Look! An ice dragon! It's on the other side of that snow arch!
Get ready for the hunt!

Flash and Fria
lead the way
down the hill.

But as the two pass under the snow arch...

Flash! The snow has blocked the entrance! We're trapped!

While on the outside...
Who fired that ray beam?
Forgive me, sire! My rifle went off accidentally.

You fool! You may have killed your queen!
I don't like this, Dale. I don't think it was an accident.

Inside the arch, the ice dragon has spotted Flash and the Queen. It slides toward them...
Quickly, Flash— Fire!

Quickly, men! Start digging! We must reach the queen.
You were too hasty, my dear Count. King Ronal suspects something.

You did it, Flash!
No, I've only stunned it... This rifle has only three charges left. We won't be able to hold it off much longer!

Flash, these dragons have a thin spot in their skulls. It's just above the eyes.
I hope you're right... Here it comes again!

Good shot, Flash, you've killed it!

Flash, darling! Thank heaven you're safe!

Prepare a sled. We'll carry the ice dragon back to the palace.

The next day, at the palace laboratory...

Ice creatures live *hundreds* of years!

From studies of these creatures, we have developed a chemical which *might* slow down the aging process in man.
Ronal and I have volunteered to test it. So far we have shown no signs of aging, nor have we felt any ill effects.
Remarkable!
Oh, Flash. We *must* try it!

My scientists think it may be fifteen or twenty years before we begin to age again.
I could never imagine you any older, Fria.
Oh, *I* can, Flash. That is why I find this experiment so interesting.

Later that evening...

Ahhhh...They are about to drink the chemical...

Oh, Flash, I feel faint!
Dale! What's wrong?

You will know soon enough, Gordon! Now, Queen Fria, I ask that you and King Ronal drink that chemical!
Traitor! What have you done?

Flash acts...

Tell me who is helping you... or *you* die too!
It was all Bellam's doing! He and Dr. Davro poisoned the chemical!

You lying coward!

Numbness is spreading through his body. Flash draws Trival's sword and faces his enemy.
Guards! Arrest that man!

No, Ronal. He's mine! He killed Dale!

Bellam fights for his life, and forces Flash toward the palace staircase.

You can't last much longer, Gordon. You're weakening already.
Before I die, I'll have the satisfaction of killing you!

Bellam rushes in for the kill. Flash gathers his remaining strength into a final thrust.

Guards are sent to arrest Dr. Davro. Flash's strength finally runs out.

I'm... getting weaker... Can hardly move...
It will pass quickly, Flash.

Davro, you!!
Yes, Flash. There was no poison.

What?
Bellam tried to pay me, but I stayed loyal to the Queen.

Instead of poison, I used a mild drug. It caused brief unconsciousness. I hoped that Bellam's helper would betray himself.

He's right. Flash,.. I feel fine.
Dale, I thought I had lost you!

The following day, their ship is loaded with the precious radium for Earth. After sad farewells, Flash and Dale leave Frigia...

Within hours, they arrive at Mingo City. Zarkov has repaired the rocketship which will carry them back to Earth.
Everything is ready, Flash. When the radium is aboard, we can take off for Earth.
It will be hard leaving Barin and Aura again.

Once again Flash, Dale, and Zarkov take leave of the planet Mongo... Mission completed!

THE MOLE MACHINE

Al Williamson
Oh, Flash! It will be good to see Zarkov again.
Yes, Dale. On the phone, the old boy sounded excited as a kid. He must have finished his project.

Hello, Doc. What have you accomplished *this* time?
Dear Zarkov!
Flash, Dale! I'm so happy you've come!

You have quite a layout here, Doc.
Yes, there are many young scientists eager to keep our country safe.

The three friends step into an elevator. It takes them 1000 feet below the surface.
In the event of nuclear war, we think human life may survive underground.

I have always wanted to explore the inner Earth. We have been working on a mole machine. It can bore through solid rock.
Now it's finished! Are you willing to test it with me, Flash?

I thought you'd never ask, Doc!
Now, just a second. Have you forgotten *me?*

No, Dale, I haven't. I don't want anyone else to know the machine is ready. We'll need you here to keep in radio contact with us.

Hmmm... Well, I don't know.
Aw, c'mon, Dale. We won't be gone for more than a few hours.

A few minutes later, inside the mole machine...
The mole uses small atomic explosions to destroy the rock ahead of it.

You win. But please be *careful*, both of you.
Good girl!

I see from the instrument panel that it can also fly through air and navigate underwater. Clever!

The mole starts its test journey, boring through solid rock.

For several miles the two explorers see nothing but rock. Then, suddenly they find themselves in an underground ocean!

...An ocean filled with many strange, threatening creatures...

KRENKELIUM

They travel several miles underwater. Then the mole emerges into an eerie world within a world...

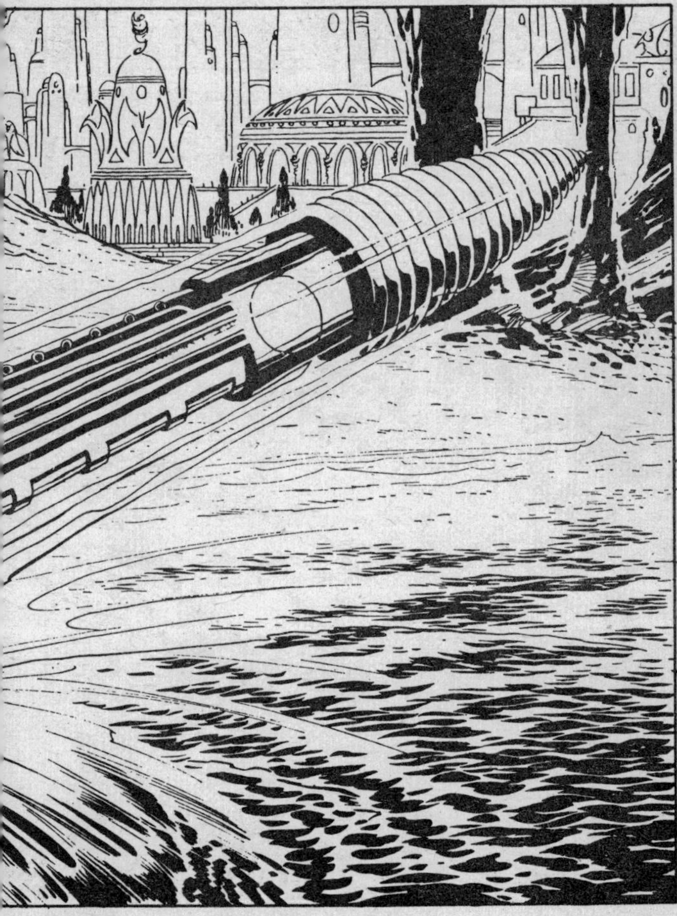

Dr. Zarkov brings the machine to a halt on the beach...
This is *fantastic*, Flash. The instruments show that the air is perfect for humans.
And that city! It *proves* that man can live underground. We *must* get a closer look!
I'll check with Dale. I'd better tell her we will probably be longer than we thought.
Good, Flash. This is a great discovery! We must explore the city.

As Flash and Zarkov leave the mole, they are being *watched*...

Zarkov! Look out!

Do not be afraid, surface men... I am Princess Darla. My father rules this world. You will not be harmed if you come quietly with us.
We come in peace. We mean no harm to you or your people.

Before Flash can reach his gun, he and Zarkov are quickly captured!
They didn't take my gun. We'll wait our chance.
Good, Flash. But let's not be hasty.

But as they approach the city...

Grabbing a spear from a frightened guard...

Flash kills the huge bird before it can harm the Princess.
You saved my life! You're a very brave man.
I hope this proves our good will.

News of Flash's deed has reached the palace...
Welcome, surface men. I am Krenko, ruler of Krenkelium. I am grateful to you for saving my daughter's life.
This is my friend, Dr. Zarkov, and I am Flash Gordon.

For your brave deed, you will be given your freedom... within Krenkelium. The machine you came in must be destroyed. If our existence becomes known on the surface, the greedy and war-like will invade us!

You mean to keep us *here* for the rest of our lives?
But we have our *own* world.
We do not permit strangers to leave here. But, come let us dine. Later we will introduce you to the wonders of krenkelium.

As Flash starts to protest,...
It is best *not* to oppose the will of my father.

Zarkov! We can't let them destroy the mole!
Don't worry, Flash, they can't get into the machine. They don't have the weapons to destroy it!

The food is *delicious*, sir... completely unlike our surface products.
Most of our food is made in our laboratories, although we have many plants which grow with-out sunlight.

Later Darla takes Flash for a stroll in the palace gardens...

Flash quickly conquers two of the attackers...

Before the third one can reach Darla...
No, Flash! Don't hurt him!

Why do you want to save them? They tried to hurt you.
Poor things...They must have escaped from the lava beds.

I don't understand.
Come, I will show you.

At the edge of the city, a fiery river of lava boils like an angry monster...
We've made these creatures slaves. They must keep building rock walls. If they did not, the lava would cover our city.

Of course, the nature of their skin makes them able to bear the terrific heat.

I wish that my father would free these poor creatures. But the very existence of our city depends upon this wall.
Darla, I think my friend, Dr. Zarkov, can help solve this problem.

Returning to the palace, Flash and Darla tell Zarkov of the lava menace...
Yes, Flash, I think there *is* a way it can be done.

Flash and Zarkov approach King Krenko with a plan...
Your highness, we are **convinced** that we can move the dangerous lava river. Please allow us to return to our ship, so that we can make preparations.

Do you take me for a *fool?* I am not fooled. You are planning to *escape!*

No, father. They are honorable men. Give them a chance...
Silence, daughter. Guards! confine these men to their quarters.

Quick, Zarkov! Head for the mole. I'll try to hold them off!
I'm going with you!

But, my child, you've put yourself in danger!

Flash slows the guards' attack.

Follow me. This is the shortest way to your ship.

But when they reach the mole, three more guards bar their way...

As Flash battles the guards, Zarkov unlocks the mole...
Thank heavens we made it! Hurry, Flash!

While Flash steers the mole machine toward the lava river, Zarkov does some quick thinking...
I've got it! We'll use the ray beams to blast a new channel for the lava river. Then it will run away from the city.

Zarkov and Flash begin the slow process of creating a new channel... and the people of Krenkelium watch in amazed silence.

The river of lava slowly begins to move away from the city, along Zarkov's new path.

The detour completed, Zarkov heads the mole back to the beach...

I don't like leaving you, Darla, after you defied your father.
I will be all right, Flash. He is a just man. He will realize you will keep your word.

But as Flash and Zarkov travel back to the surface of Earth, they know that some day they will return to the underground city of Krenkelium!

THE END

THE DEATH

TRAP of MONGO
Flash Gordon! Everywhere I turn... *Flash Gordon!* His deeds clog the screen!
Control yourself, Gorlak!
Though long absent from the planet Mongo, Flash Gordon is remembered. The legend of his daring continues to be told... to all who enjoy the freedom he helped win... and, to some who do not!

I hate Flash Gordon!

His peace and democracy have ruined Mongo! What life is this for a born warrior and nobleman?
Control, Gorlak,. The day is at hand!

For years this fortress has been our world ...training, preparing, waiting... Now, it is *time*.
But... Flash Gordon is on Earth! As long as he lives, Mongo can never *truly* be ours!

The preparations are complete! I can *promise* Flash Gordon's return!
You've completed the machine? Small wonder you're called wizard... I must see it *now!*

And as the wizard prepares to demonstrate his latest invention, so too does Dr. Hans Zarkov, on Earth.

Go ahead, Dale ... take the car. Give the mad scientist a chance to show his wares!
Fine! But don't expect me to go very far!
That'll serve to demonstrate until we can test the beamer's full range...

But the beamer is to be given a far greater test, as Dale steps outside the laboratory...
Flash!
Zarkov! Stop the test! Something's gone wrong!
It's some kind of outside force...Not my equipment!

She's gone...V-Vanished! What kind of devilish force could do that?
The instruments are going crazy! But I'm still getting a faint signal!

Dale! N-NO, Dale!

Dale's beamer is still working?!
Great Scott! If these readings are correct... That beam's coming from... *Mongo!!*

B-But the people of Mongo are our friends... Why would *they* kidnap Dale?
We helped bring them freedom, Flash... There will always be an evil few who resent it!

Doc, we've got to get back there... *Quickly!* If Dale's in the hands of some madman...
I've always felt we'd return to Mongo again... But never under conditions as unpleasant as these.

...That's why I've kept our ship ready and waiting!
Zarkov, you're a wonder!

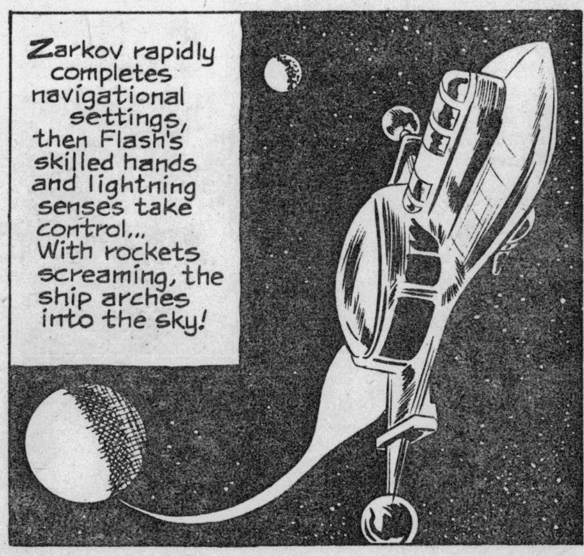
Zarkov rapidly completes navigational settings, then Flash's skilled hands and lightning senses take control... With rockets screaming, the ship arches into the sky!

Finally they land at Mingo City Rocket Port,..

Down with the strangers! Destroy their ship!
Stick close, Doc: They're completely berserk!

Flash Gordon! Dr. Zarkov! This way!
It's one of the palace guards!

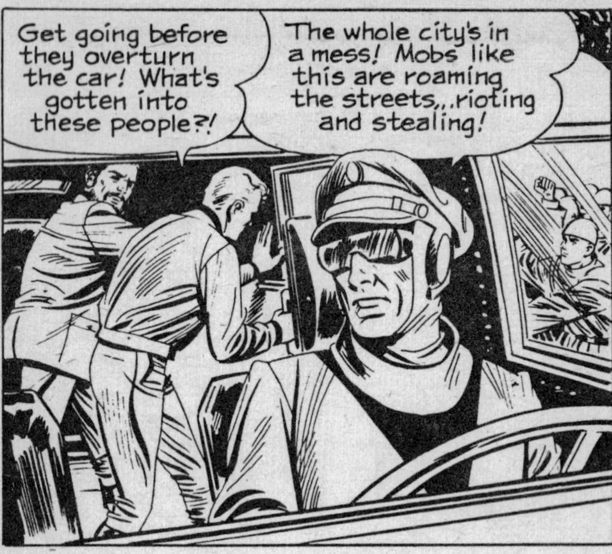
Get going before they overturn the car! What's gotten into these people?!
The whole city's in a mess! Mobs like this are roaming the streets,..rioting and stealing!

But, King Barin... the council... Why haven't they stopped this?
Vanished... All but Queen Aura! Agents spread panic... Rumors of revolution... Even the army's divided!

Inside the royal palace, the Queen greets the two Earthmen...

What if he holds Dale and the others? No army can pierce his mountain fortress!
No army.. But perhaps two men... We must act quickly, before his troops reach here!

As night falls, a jet launch hovers silently over the dark forest surrounding the mountain...
This is as close as we dare get... The rest is up to the gliding capes... and fate!

As you said, wizard, They're into the forest—right on schedule! Prepare the girl,.....in case Gordon gets this far!
And throw away her silly beaming device... It's already served our purpose!

Moat's too wide...one of the patrols will spot us before we make it across!
unless some-thing takes their attention..

Suddenly the scientist springs forth, blazing stun-rays from his blaster!
...Like this!

Got to keep 'em busy till Flash gets his chance!

Too late to help Zarkov! Mustn't let his sacrifice go to waste!

Strong strokes carry the powerful Earthman through the moat's murky depths...
Something ahead... Some kind of drain or entrance...

...keep something in!!

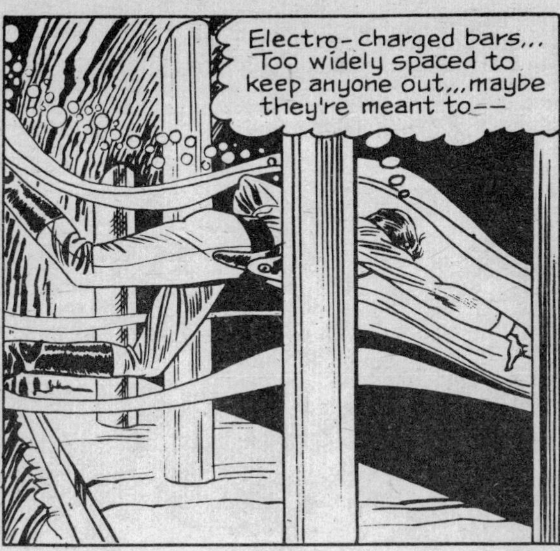
Electro-charged bars... Too widely spaced to keep anyone out,,, maybe they're meant to--

Shark-lizard! Only one chance...

Flashing rows of razor-teeth thrash madly at the human target, as the giant reptile streaks for the kill...
If this doesn't work, I'll never get *another* try!

Got him! He'll be stunned until I'm out of here!

Even as Flash escapes the shark-lizard, Zarkov is brought to Gorlak...
Fools! Don't bother me with underlings! I want *Flash Gordon!* Place this one in the dungeon with the other council members.
One moment, Gorlak...

This is Zarkov, a scientific genius! I can use him in my laboratory..
Then *take* him! I wait only to humble the Earthling, Gordon!

Zarkov is taken to the wizard's lab...
This can teleport captives by breaking down their molecular structure into light particles and re-assembling them here...
Beaming to Earth strained its capacities.. ...Your genius could convert it to unlimited power!

Before you refuse, I might point out your alternative... a swim in the grotto of the shark-lizard!
I-I'll do what I can...
While I'm alive, there's a slim hope I can act!

Meanwhile, Flash continues his attempt to penetrate Gorlak's fortress...
That grotto was nearly a dead end... This tower window should make for a safer entrance...

Muscles aching from the long climb, Flash pulls himself into the window to see...
Dale!

Only one way to reach her from here,.. jump!
But as Flash's boots strike the floor, the hiss of moving ropes knifes the air,..

The net draws tight, as Flash pulls loose the bonds holding his sweetheart,.
Oh, Flash, darling! If only I could have warned you!

What th--a net! The whole floor's coming up at me,.. It's a plastic net!

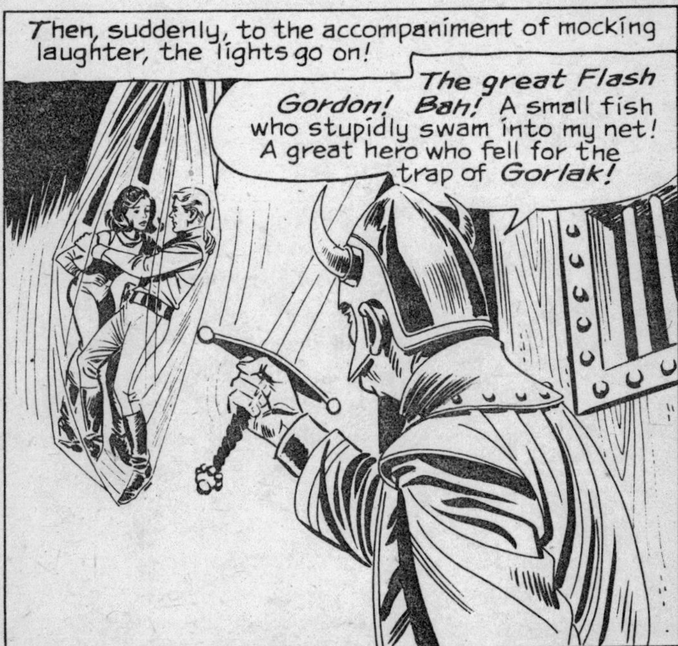
Then, suddenly, to the accompaniment of mocking laughter, the lights go on!
The great Flash Gordon! Bah! A small fish who stupidly swam into my net! A great hero who fell for the trap of Gorlak!

I've waited years for this, Flash Gordon! Now, *face Gorlak!*

The door is locked from the outside... Here is a weapon... We're alone, Earthling! *Face me!*
Flash, you've done too much already... He's fresher than you!

Surrender if you like, or fight! Either way, these cameras will beam my triumph to every visi-screen in Mongo! The whole republic will see you *crawl!*

Save your breath, Gorlak! You're going to need it for the fight!

While the clashing swords echo from visi-screens throughout the fortress and the land, Zarkov makes a desperate plan,..

And in the tower cell, Gorlak presses his attack,..
Time on Earth has rusted your skill,.. How easily I disarm you!
He's a blow-hard, but he's good! Got to keep moving before he -

Wizard ran out to stop Gorlak, guard's watching the screen... ...I can aim the transmitter on the dungeon cell holding Barin and the others... Got to act *now!*

--Gets me!
That was the *flat* of my sword. Once down, you'll taste the edge... *and death!*

Flash's hands claw the floor, striking... a piece of netting!
We have a saying on Earth: Down--

--But not out!
UGGGHHHHHH!

Oh, Flash..
Don't look! He fell on his own sword...
No matter! You saved *me* the trouble... The fool has served his purpose!

T-The wizard.. He's really...
Ming the Merciless!
You dared think the supreme intelligence was defeated forever? For years I've worked in secret *for this moment!*

Without a leader, Mingo City will fall to Gorlak's men... and me!
As for you, Flash Gordon... I had planned a thousand deaths. Now, face to face, I know there can be but one way...

No use... Can't break his hold... Fight with Gorlak took everything I had... Maybe... I can get off... one last...

Every fiber of his being... Every ounce of courage... boils up to a final effort...
...PUNCH!

But one blow, even the mightiest, cannot stop Ming the Merciless for long...
Guards! Quickly! Stop them!
Flash, we're too late! They're blocking our way!

I'll chance no more delays... Destroy them! Now!

Then, before they can squeeze a blast from their ray guns...
The matter transmitter!

And in the laboratory, the matter transmitter completes its task...

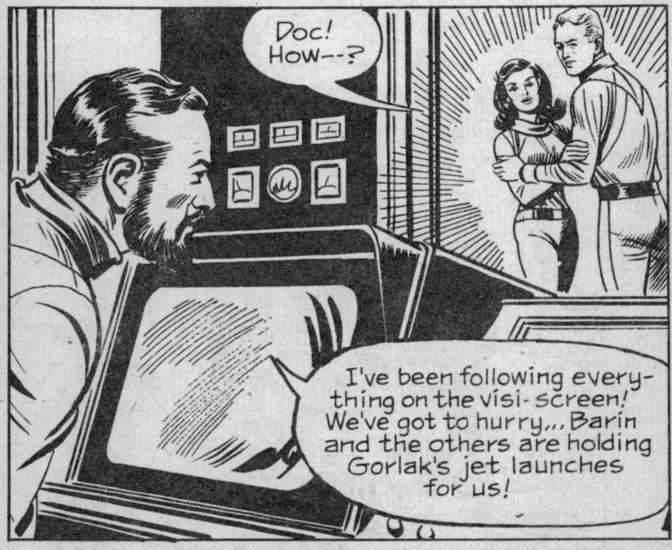

You freed the council members with that same machine? The matter transmitter?
The same machine that snatched Dale,.. And the same machine I've left *booby-trapped* for Ming!

As the jet launches soar into the dawn sky...

Thank Tao! I was afraid you wouldn't make it...The launches are all warmed up!
We'll take the small one! See you back in Mingo City!

Looks like they found your surprise, Zarkov!

When the council gets back, Mingo City will soon be cleared of Gorlak's troops...
But we can't be certain that we finished Ming!

This time we'll stay on Mongo until any new threat of Ming's tyranny is ended... *forever!*
THE END